How Do Dinosaurs

Get Well Soon?

EUOPLOCEPHALUS

CARNOTAURUS

TROPEOGNATHUS

PARASAUROLOPHUS

BRACHIOSAURUS

DILOPHOSAURUS

GALLIMIMUS

STYRACOSAURUS

VELOCIRAPTOR

TUOJIANGOSAURUS

EUOPLOCEPHALUS

CARNOTAURUS

TROPEOGNATHUS

PARASAUROLOPHUS

BRACHIOSAURUS

DILOPHOSAURUS

GALLIMIMUS

STYRACOSAURUS

VELOCIRAPTOR

TUOJIANGOSAURUS

JANE YOLEN

How Do Dinosaurs

Get Well Soon?

Illustrated by

MARK TEAGUE

SCHOLASTIC INC.

New York   Toronto   London   Auckland   Sydney
Mexico City   New Delhi   Hong Kong   Buenos Aires

This book was originally published in hardcover
by the Blue Sky Press in 2003.

ISBN 0-439-24101-4

Text copyright © 2003 by Jane Yolen.
Illustrations copyright © 2003 by Mark Teague.
Published by Scholastic Inc. SCHOLASTIC and
associated logos are trademarks and/or
registered trademarks of Scholastic Inc.

12 11 10 9 8 7 6 5 4   4 5 6 7 8 9/0

Printed in the U.S.A.   08

Designed by Kathleen Westray
First Scholastic paperback printing, January 2004

To David Francis Stemple, my first grandson

J. Y.

To Bonnie and Robbie, for dreaming of dinosaurs

M. T.

What if a dinosaur
catches the flu?

Does he whimper and whine
in between each *Atchoo*?

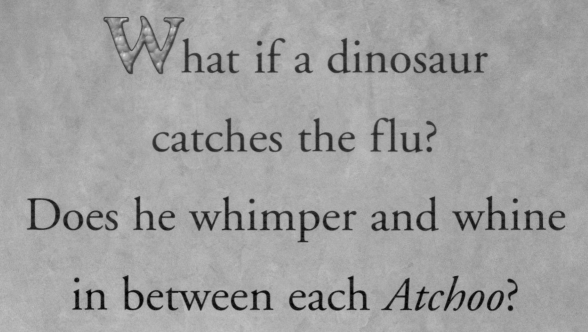

Does he drop

dirty tissues

all over

the floor?

GALLIMIMUS

Does he fling
all his medicine
out of the door?

Does he flip off
his covers
with tooth
and with tail?

EUOPLOCEPHALUS

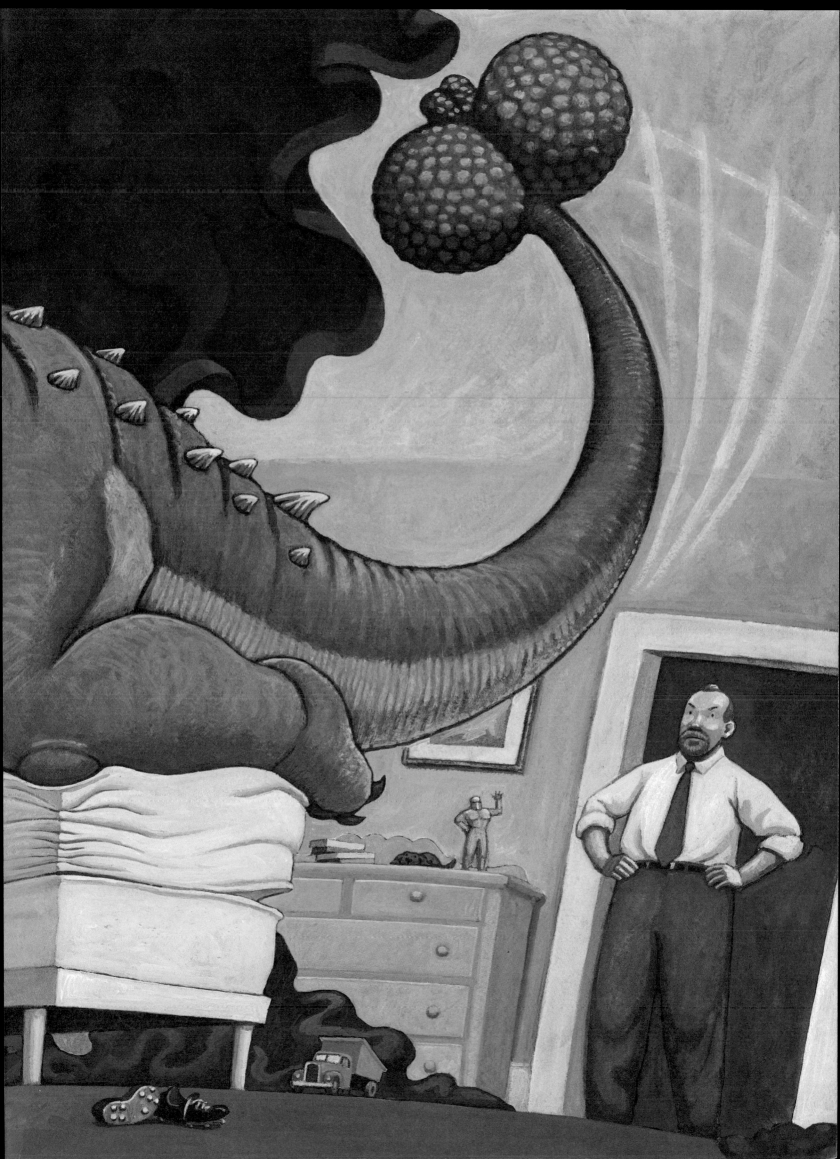

Does he
dump out
his juice
and get sick
in a pail?

BRACHIOSAURUS

DILOPHOSAURUS

DOES A

DINOSAUR

WAIL?

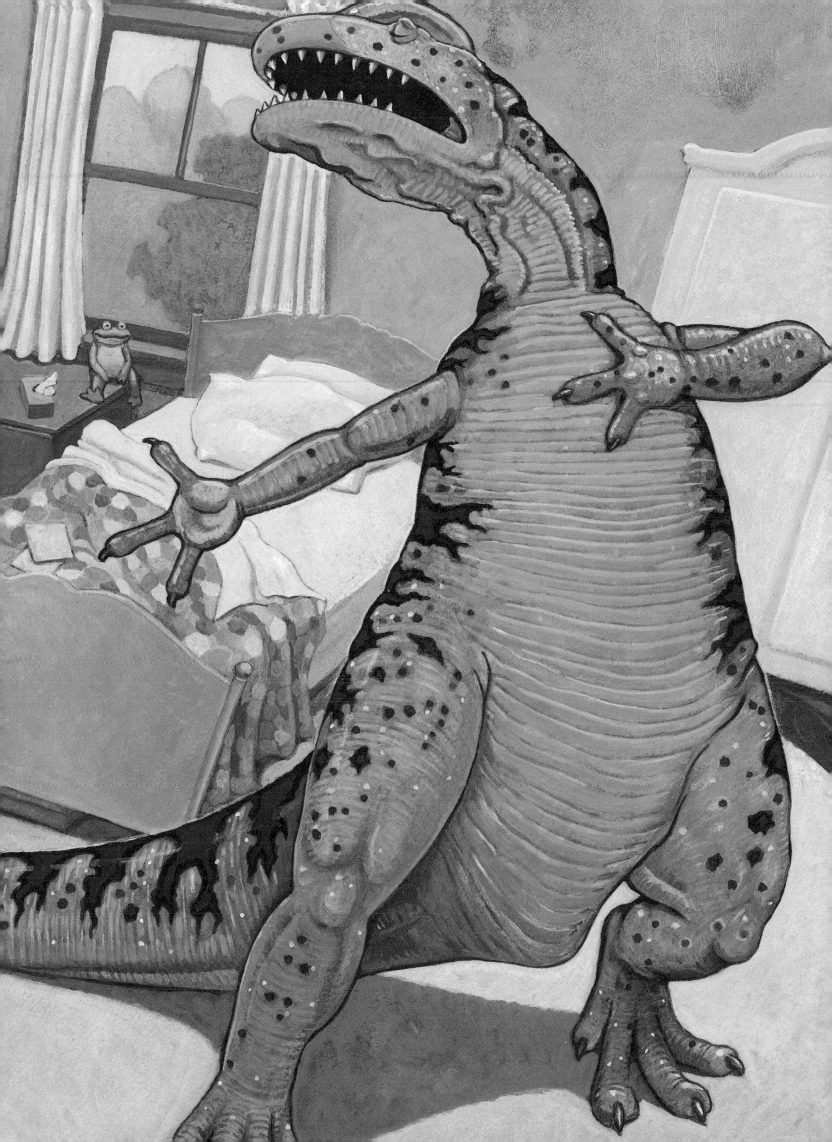

What if a dinosaur
goes to the doc?

Does he drag all his feet

till his mom is in shock?

CARNOTAURUS

Does he hold
his mouth closed
when he's told,
"Open wide"?

Does he scream?

Is he mean?

Does he run off

and hide?

Does he

push back each drink,

spit his pills in the sink?

Does he

make a big stink?

Is that what you think?

No . . .

He drinks lots of juice,
and he gets lots of rest.
He's good at the doctor's,
'cause doctors know best.

He uses a hankie
on mouth
and on nose.
He snuggles
right down
underneath
the bedclothes.

VELOCIRAPTOR

He takes all his medicine

without a fight.

DIPLODOCUS

He closes his eyes.

He whispers good night.

Then Mama and Papa

tiptoe out the door.

Get well.

Get well, little dinosaur.

EUOPLOCEPHALUS

CARNOTAURUS

TROPEOGNATHUS

PARASAUROLOPHUS

BRACHIOSAURUS

DILOPHOSAURUS

GALLIMIMUS

STYRACOSAURUS

VELOCIRAPTOR

TUOJIANGOSAURUS